MW00946525

> Chips & Threads is dedicated to the
> Memory of Amy Bohr McClure
> 1964 - 2020

To Ann
We love you very much.
Enjoy this little book.

Tuck

Dearest Ann,
   I think of you often and
hope you are well. I hope you
enjoy this cute book. Much love.

Sarah Sanders

CHIPS & THREADS

Written by Tuck McClure

Illustrated by Sarah Sanders

Once upon a time, there was a beautiful valley with a broad river flowing through. On one side of the valley lived a woodcutter named Chips. No one knew if he had another name and no one cared.

They always knew who it was when they saw him coming. They could only see this great cloud of woodchips coming up the road with a cart filled with firewood pulled by an ox.

The ox had only one horn and
one eye and he always followed
behind without a lead. If the ox
could talk he would tell you he
had lost his horn and his eye in
a battle.

He knew it was important but
he could not remember what it
was about or which ox it was
with. Battles are like that you
know. The why is forgotten,
but the eye and the horn
don't come back.

2

Chips had the best firewood in the valley. It was dry and well split.
Everyone in the valley bought firewood from Chips.

When he came he always left
the wood by the gate, because no
one would let him in their yard, much
less in their house. They would never be
able to clean up all those chips.

On the other side of the valley lived a seamstress named Threads. No one knew if she had another name and no one cared. They always knew who it was when they saw her coming.

They could only see this colorful cloud of little bits of thread and fabric coming up the road pulling a little wagon with beautiful jackets in it.

She always left the jacket by the gate, because
no one would let her in their yard, much less
in their house. They would never be able to
clean up all those little bits of threads!

Every lady in the valley bought
their jackets from Threads.
The outsides were very nice,
and the linings were really
beautiful.

One sunny day Threads went to
a nice spot by the river to sew
a lining in a jacket.

Across the river she could see where the big logging company had cut down all the trees and hauled away the logs. She began to hear the buzz of a tiny saw. Then she saw this cloud of chips moving slowly through the old limbs. The cloud seemed to turn and look across the river.

9

On the same sunny day Chips began to cut firewood from a place where the big logging company had cut down all the trees and hauled away the logs. As he straightens up from cutting a log, he saw this cloud of threads across the river. It seemed to be looking at him.

11

As if some power had taken hold of him, he stepped into the river and started to wade across. He knew the river well.

He knew where to walk so it would never get over his chest. He walked in the river drawn by the power of the shiny cloud of threads.

The clouds met at the stones on the side of the river. Their edges blended into a new color that cannot be described.

A hand came from the center of each cloud reaching for the other. Ten fingers entwined. A single cloud of chips and threads swirling and glowing.

Chips and Threads now united walk out the valley.

14

The old ox with one horn and one eye comes out of the river pulling his cart of wood. He follows behind, he never needed a lead.

If you like us: Facebook us, Instagram us, Snapshot us

Thank you

clips, Threads &

Available on Amazon & at Barnes and Nobel

Web Page https://www.chipsandthreadsbook.com/